THE DEATH CATCHER

MATT RIDENOUR

ISBN-10:0615941117
ISBN-13:9780615941110

DEDICATION

To my friends and family who have supported me throughout the years.
You know who you are.

CONTENTS

ACKNOWLEDGMENTS

A special thanks to those who helped me develop my craft, voice, and style; to those who have both boosted my self-esteem and torn it down when necessary; to those who continue to survive my eccentricities and keep me encouraged through both rough and restful times.

1 THE CONTRACT

Razio traced the gold trim on his black cape and gazed ahead, studying the innocents he would soon murder. Duty and gold. Lots of gold. He tried to convince himself that nothing else mattered. After tugging a handful of his cape's silk in anger and guilt, he lowered himself into the stalks of wheat hiding him and his three mercenaries. He squeezed his eyes shut to still his soul. No. He would never find peace. Not in this life.

Forcing his eyes open, Razio made himself concentrate on the contract.

Cloudless rays drew sweat from his forehead as soft eddies hissed through the wheat, swaying the stalks as he kneeled firmly. He frowned at the naïve farmers and shoved down the knots of emotion at his task, then shook his head. Usually, mercenaries never dared venture this close to the border. They risked crossing paths with a Creator. Then again, that's why he'd been called. Nobody was safe in the midst of a Death Catcher. Razio sighed as the soft sways of nature blew his brown hooks of hair across his forehead.

Next to him, Darium tapped the pommel of his sword with a bony finger, and whispered, "What are we waiting for? Let's get this done. We've been tracking them all day." The fool bobbed his wrinkled head over the wheat to glare at the farmers with twisted anticipation.

Razio curled his lip and touched the jagged knife in his belt. "Get down. Be quiet. You know what we're looking for. I haven't sensed anything yet."

"That's because the Creator isn't here." Darium wiped sweat off his bald head with the palm of his hand as the other two mercenaries nodded, mumbling agreement.

"Trust me, you don't want to risk it." Razio turned his gaze back upon the men harvesting in the field. At least there were no women or children. He closed his eyes and gulped down his guilt. Yes, it had to be done. Otherwise, there would be no end to this war. Besides, it was nothing he hadn't done before. Many times before. He stroked his forming beard with the back of his hand. It was difficult to believe he'd survived so long.

Darium grumbled. "Well, whatever you need to do, do it. I hate being this close to the border."

Razio couldn't disagree. But it was risky to use the powers of the dead near Creators. They could sense it. He touched one of the gold symbols on his cape with a finger. It translated, Wariness Begets Reason. He'd followed that lesson from the day of his ascension. It hadn't failed him yet, but he had to do more than wait. The Creator hid himself too well—couldn't be found by normal means. And time was running out.

Fortunately, in the middle of a war, there was no shortage of burial grounds. There should be one just beyond the wheat field.

Steadying his hand, Razio relaxed his tense muscles and cleared his mind. Time to fulfill his obligation. Reaching into his soul, Razio touched his Ashima—the rare link connecting him to the power of creation itself—and drew in a breath through his nose. Like always, the suddenness stole the wind from his lungs.

He clenched his jaw and tightened his fists, struggling to contain the pain threatening to tear him apart. It roared through his veins, seared through his flesh, heightened senses changing his perception. The amplified nuttiness of the wheat and rancid sweat of his comrades filled his nostrils. The beat of the afternoon sun scorched his neck and the back of his hands. Low whispers of those poor innocents echoed in his ears as the men cut with their scythes, preparing the wheat to be threshed.

Razio forced himself to focus, pushing the familiar pain away, but as a trained Death Catcher, he'd been tainted by the dead. Now, he could only use the link of his Ashima to harness the power of the dead, stealing the essence that belonged to the world below.

Steadying his senses, he reached beyond the fields with his Ashima, past the farmers, wheat field, and surrounding homes, searching for the dead.

The fresh ones were best to use—always the most potent. Ah, just beyond the ridge. The dead prickled him through the link. The power crackled and hissed, leaking from the empty flesh and bone—a mass grave from a recent battle.

Reaching out with his Ashima, Razio touched the sizzling power of the bodies, mingling with it, melding with it, leeching the spicy, popping energy, turning the remains of the cadavers into dust and building his Ashima with that ever-familiar pressure, which the first Death Catchers had dubbed "reservoir."

Now, to find his mark.

Razio scanned the fields, weaved his power through the innocents, but nothing. Perhaps Darium was right. He shook his head at that thought. No, his contact had been clear. This was the location. He just had to try harder.

After exhaling another breath, he flecked out his power, dotting all life with the mark of the dead. Ah, there it was. The Creator had failed to clean his trail. Razio sniffed. Most Creators underestimated Death Catchers.

It would seem this one was no exception. He recombined his power, focusing it on the tracks of life the Creator had left behind. He followed it to the back of the field behind the innocents, into the barn, then finally, into the ground. Razio smiled. This one was more intelligent than the others. But he'd never known a Creator to hide. Something was different. Something was wrong.

Regardless, he must ensure he drew no notice. He raised a fist and whispered, "Steady, now. He's here, hiding in a hole beneath the barn."

Darium sniffed. "Cowering like a beast."

Razio snapped back, "Do not underestimate him. He's there for a reason. One your fool mind cannot comprehend."

Darium tapped a sarcastic fist to his heart in mock salute. "Yes, sir! Of course, sir!"

Razio curled his lip. When he finished this commitment, he'd request a fresh batch of mercenaries. He despised this bunch. Might even kill them if given the opportunity. "Move in. Do not let them see you. Be quick. Be silent." He pointed at the farmers with his hand, signaling the squad into action.

This was the part Razio hated. He'd been a soldier, a great soldier. But with his talents, his superiors had deemed him too exceptional to risk in open combat. And being but a soldier, he had followed procedure up until his commanding officer had given him his official discharge papers, and then after when ordered to head up a band of mercenaries on special assignment. He hadn't questioned or disagreed, it was more gold after all. Much more. But at the time, he hadn't realized the cost to his soul. Now, all he did was track down stragglers and their rare Creators, then kill them if they didn't submit to his Lord's rule. And according to Razio's source, these farmers had not submitted. These innocent, civilian farmers.

But who was he to question? He loved his country, trusted his leaders. Even if everything felt wrong…

Shaking his head, Razio watched his squad crawl through the wheat field, and traced another gold symbol on his black cape—one of his most recent commendations. He held his breath a moment to force down his emotion. They would take care of the farmers. Time to fulfill his end of the contract. He couldn't wait to rid himself of his ignorant band of killers.

He silenced his footsteps with a wisp of his acquired power, then tucked his heavy shoulders low and sprinted through the field. The tufts of wheat instantly decayed at his touch—falling to the ground as soundless ash. The wind whipped past his face, blowing in his ears as he raced through the field, around his squad, then behind the farmers. He was careful not to draw any more attention. He just hoped the Creator hadn't been actively searching for the signs of a Death Catcher.

When the barn came into sight, it hit him—the first scream. But he couldn't look back, couldn't regret what he had ordered. It was the farmers' faults, wasn't it? They'd known what would happen.

Another scream. Then another. Unable to bear the torment, Razio stopped at the rear of the barn and kneeled, using his cape to mask his emotion. He was a Death Catcher. A good soldier. Why did he feel this way? It should have grown easier after the first time, or the second, or even the twentieth or thirtieth, but it hadn't. Those screams haunted him when all else was silent. The faces of those he'd murdered sneered at him in his dreams.

Razio balled his fists then rose high to his feet. The Creator. That's why he was here. He closed his eyes, stretching out his Ashima, using the powers he had acquired to ensure there were no surprises. Surely, the Creator had heard the screams.

Yes, there he was. The fool hadn't even moved. But, Razio sensed something. Something different. Wary, he threaded the tendrils of the dead in front of him to search for any portent, then finding none, stepped towards the entrance to the barn.

The door stood open, and inside, he saw stalks of wheat piled high on either side, that nutty aroma even thicker here, layered with mildew from old straw and rain. Hay bales and yarn—strung about in spools—leaned against the mounds and lay scattered across the floor. But in the center, the solid, wooden door to below had been left cracked open, and no yarn, neither hay nor wheat rested upon it. Here, the Creator would take his final breath, then meet the Lost Winds in the next life.

Razio let out a deep breath, then strode towards the door.

Not a pace away, the door to below creaked. Razio tensed, holding his pulsating power at bay, expecting something but not knowing what. He licked his teeth, readying his reflexes, tapping his fingertips with his thumbs, prepared to release the dead at a heartbeat's notice. The pressure pounded at the walls of his Ashima, struggling for release.

He took one more step. A flash of light ignited an explosion, blowing the door off its hinges and igniting the bales of hay and wheat. Half-blind, Razio found himself sailing through the barn, ears buzzing, air ripped from his lungs. When he landed, he skidded back towards the entrance through blazing wheat and straw, his flesh burning with agony. When wind finally returned to his lungs, he screamed with pain, but could not hear his own cry—his anger and agony at odds with each other. How had the Creator been quicker? It should have been impossible.

Then in the midst of the flame, from the origin of the explosion, a man draped with red robes stepped up from below. Cinders and ash flaked down from the scorching wheat as he rose, but none of it touched him—like drops of water slithering across a river of oil. Long and sharp black hair clawed down from his head in neat lines, and if the explosion hadn't bespoken his intent, his cutting eyes would have. With a growl, he said, "You will not have him."

There was nobody else here, was there? Razio coughed, gasping to catch his breath, his stinging flesh burning where the explosion had touched it. His ears still rang, but the powers of the dead were healing him. Quickly, Razio checked the pressure of his reservoir, then coughed again. The blast had taken out most of his defenses, but he still had some left. He cracked his knuckles. It would have to be enough.

With effort, he rose to his feet, then spat. "I came for you, Creator."

The enemy curled his lip with hunger. "My name is Voltium."

As expected, the fool raged forward, twisting his hands, summoning his Ashima to create a spell. This time, Razio was prepared. He smiled with anticipation. Quick or not, it appeared this Creator was not accustomed to battling Death Catchers. The pratter should have ended it when he had the chance.

The air churned, swirling with the formation of the Creator's power. It crackled as it sparked to life. But Razio had seen this spell before–deadly if released, but slow to build. He growled, then used the dwindling powers of the dead to twist the spell back into itself. As the pressure of his reservoir deflated, his heightened senses diminished.

When the spell dissipated, Voltium glared, and fueled it with more of his Ashima–then narrowed his sharp eyes and clawed at the air.

9

Razio growled, then pushed out more of his reservoir. He tensed his shoulders, balled his fists, struggling to gain the upper hand. Fool spell or not, this Creator was strong. Voltium fought back, gritting his teeth, digging his nails into his palms, but Razio persevered. Sweat trickled down his neck, his face grew hot with the effort. Who was this Creator? Who was he protecting?

The power of the dead continued to ebb. The smoking barn creaked under its own weight and started collapsing, ash and burning cinders drifting down around him. His reservoir almost dry, Razio knew he couldn't fight much longer. Head faint, knees weak, he unsheathed the knife from his belt. If he couldn't defeat him with the dead, perhaps a simple blade would do.

He staggered forward, and Voltium seemed not to notice—too focused on that deadly spell. Perhaps he had a chance. Perhaps this Creator was too overconfident to perceive a simple knife as a threat.

Now within a pace, he caught Voltium's gaze. The Creator's eyes widened, and Razio tightened his grip. He lunged forward with the blade, and having spent himself, the Creator made a feeble attempt to deflect it away, missing. The knife slipped into Voltium's chest to the hilt, and the Creator gasped. Blood spilled over his red robes, spurted across Razio's hands and face. It tasted like metal.

Razio quickly spat it out. It was all he could do to stand. The Creator fell to the ground with a final moan, and the spell fizzled into the burning air. Razio sighed with relief. It had been a long time since he'd faced such a challenge. He'd been lucky.

Trusses of the razed barn splintered. Smoke stung his eyes. The heat of the fire tested the limits of his strength. He needed to leave. Now.

Just as Razio turned, he spotted movement. The Creator had been carrying something in a pack. Interesting, perhaps that's what he'd been protecting.

With curious instinct, Razio grabbed the pack, sheathed his knife after hurriedly wiping off the blood, and struggled out of the barn. Once out, he sucked in the fresh, cool air, relief washing over him. He limped as far away as he could bear, vaguely wondering about his idiot men, but more curious about the pack and its contents. He collapsed to the ground with a sigh near the edge of the wheat field, relieved to have finally defeated his mark.

But how long could he continue doing this? He'd murdered so many men to satisfy the hunger of his Lord and self-proclaimed King. Razio curled his lip at the thought, felt his stomach wrench to the back of his throat. Each killing hurt worse than the last. How did the others manage it with such ease? Yes, his hands more deftly snatched lives away with each murder, but the weight, the cost, the burden to his soul…

Razio blinked, struggling to control his emotion, then returned his gaze to the pack. It had caught his attention by moving in the barn. Perhaps a prized pet? A familiar?

He furrowed his brow, then unwrapped the twine binding it. He struggled with the knots, then finally cut them loose with his knife, and peered inside.

Razio gasped.

A baby. Wrapped in nothing but a cloth and a blanket. He blinked. When but a child, Razio had seen a baby, but in no other time in his life. This didn't make sense. Something so small shouldn't have survived. It hadn't even cried.

Razio knuckled his brow. He knew the orders. It didn't matter—man, woman, child. Baby. His Lord had sentenced each of them to death. And soldiers followed orders.

Blade still in Razio's grasp, he eased it with shaking hands closer to the infant. This couldn't be any different. It was still human, big or small, and the orders were clear.

He inched the knife closer still, until the blade touched its tiny neck.

At that moment, the baby smiled at him—the gaze pure and sweet. Deep and alive.

Razio froze, unable to breathe. He couldn't remember the last time he'd felt alive. That one look burst open all his brimming guilt and pain, impelled forth the emotional horrors caused by his past commanders' orders and worse—what they hadn't ordered. In that moment, anger and regret bled out of his soul into the fields. He now recognized himself for what he was. His attention locked on the infant's pure smile, foreign tenderness began reaching up from the recesses of his soul.

Tears touched the corners of his eyes. This infant's sweet and innocent life-bearing gaze bore deeper than any blade could. This child needed to love, to be loved.

He dropped the knife, cradled the baby close to his chest, and struggled to hold back tears, shaking with remorse. A moment ago, he had intended to murder a child. Razio shook his head and clenched his jaw. He used to be a good man.

It hit him harder than the explosion. He'd been fighting for the wrong side. Who could carry out such orders?

Not him. Not anymore.

He swallowed his tears and stared again at the baby—its eyes burrowing hope into his soul. Such a wonder. Such a precious spark of life.

Without regard for his men, the wheat field, or the world itself, Razio slung the pack over his shoulders, held the baby close to his chest, and strode through the grassy plane towards his horse. Nothing mattered except this child.

Not a dozen paces away, a voice growled from behind, "What are you doing with that? Give it to me."

Startled, he turned and glared. The shadowy form of a man hid half the setting sun. Razio had to squint to see him.

The voice was confident, without remorse, without care. "I said, give it to me. You're done here. Your men are dead. I killed them. And we have orders." Simply a fact. A long, black cape decorated with gold symbols flitted in the wind. A Death Catcher.

Razio grimaced, then turned on shaky legs, still clutching the soundless baby to his chest. "No. This is my mark. My contract. And it is fulfilled." He'd taken too long. Wanting the reward, another band of mercenaries must have found the Creator, and disappointed, had killed Razio's men. Normally, it wouldn't have mattered. He hadn't liked them anyway. Besides, he'd already killed the Creator. But all contracts were clear. No survivors. No hostages.

The Death Catcher sneered, his straw-blond hair unmoving in the pale wind. "Not yet."

Razio slowly smiled. Both of them understood. This would be the first contract he'd ever broken. And his last.

But he couldn't fight this Death Catcher. He only had enough power left for one burst, and it would take minutes to re-feed on the dead. Minutes too long. He needed to run. Razio narrowed his eyes, then studied the wheat field. A Death Catcher never rode alone. It takes time and concentration to aquire the dead, leaving them vulnerable for that short while. And a lucky bow shot at the wrong time could take even the greatest of Death Catchers. Where were his men?

Ah, razing the barns in the distance. He hid his recognition and held the baby tighter. Razio wore the worst grimace he could muster, then growled, "It's not up to you to decide. Leave me. Now. Or fall to the Lost Winds like my men." He prepared what was left of his power in case he needed it. Would his bluff work? This Death Catcher's cape had close to the amount of golden symbols emblazoned upon it, but still, fewer than his. Razio should be stronger–well, stronger when both were at full reserve.

The Death Catcher drew his lips together in thought, measuring the value of Razio's words. It was impossible to gauge another's reservoir, but if they fell into combat, one of them would die. Razio.

"If you leave, you will be hunted. Hunted by us all."

Not allowing a reaction, he glared at the Death Catcher, hiding his nerves, then turned back towards his horse. He must not walk too quickly, nor slowly. He couldn't appear weak.

Once on his horse, he rubbed the baby's back–who stared up at him with dependent crystal-blue eyes. Loving eyes. But he could feel the Death Catcher's glare boring into his skull. Regardless, Razio would soon be named a traitor. For choosing not to murder a child. He shook his head, almost spitting in revulsion. How had he not seen it?

Razio should have turned from the new empire Tynza sooner. He'd been but a child at its inception, and he'd grown to love it. But with his mounting patriotism, his callousness had slowly progressed over years of soldiering. His ascension to Death Catcher hadn't helped–even worsened the guilt.

Razio clenched his jaw. Though all who fought for his Lord claimed him to be the glorious savior of this era, this newly forming country had been forged with innocent blood. He was the enemy. It had taken this infant to wake him from his slumber of shadow and death.

Again, the baby smiled, and Razio felt his resolve renew tenfold. Holding the child close with one arm, he heeled his horse to a gallop before the Death Catcher had a chance to change his mind.

2 THE INNOCENT

Grass and wheat flew by in a dizzy flurry as the horse continued galloping. He'd ridden at least a few leagues, and so far, Razio hadn't sensed anything. It might be a good sign, but there was no telling how far word had spread. He glanced down at the baby, who'd fallen asleep to the rhythm of the horse's hooves. "You'll be all right. You'll see." But the question remained–where was he going?

No way he'd ride back to Tynza. Even if he disguised himself as a farmer, the other Death Catchers would find and murder him and the baby. Razio knew–it wasn't the baby that mattered to the others, but the act of defiance. As a Death Catcher himself, one of the best, he was master of their methods. Death Catchers could track anything. In numbers, they were unstoppable. So where, then? If he managed to squeeze past Psynops–the city of Creators–he'd need to ride either over the mountains or through the desert. Razio dug his heels into his horse with frustration. Half the

17

strongest men couldn't survive either path, so how could an infant? Besides, he hadn't the provisions to last.

He sniffed. Word of a rogue Death Catcher carrying a baby would spread faster than any man could ride.

There was only one option–Psynops itself. Razio grumbled. He'd just killed a Creator, and now he was running to them for help? Ridiculous, but it was his only chance. The child's only chance.

"Hooah!" Razio snapped his reins and steered his mount north towards the border–just days away. If his Lord got his way, which he would, all this land would soon be nothing but barren waste–a hard barrier between Tynza and Psynops. And then, Razio was certain the power-hungry rising emperor would turn his eyes south to the Sovereign Lands.

Razio now understood why all the innocents resisted, even when faced with certain death. Their hope of future generations, the need to protect those who could not protect themselves. But there still seemed to be another reason–a reason he couldn't yet grasp.

Drawing closer to the border of Psynops, ear-piercing screech not unlike a baby hawk made Razio move for his knife. He halted his mount, then horrified by the sound screeching from the child's mouth, held the infant away at arms length, and found himself soaked in baby urine. "No, baby, no. What have you done? What is that noise?"

The baby continued to scream, a thing of pure agony. Razio grimaced, watching with disgust as the urine continued dripping down. "Shh, quiet. What is wrong with you?"

But it didn't stop. His stomach cramped in panic, and his skin grew hot. He looked from side to side, but there was no help—only scarce trees in the grasslands and diminishing wheat fields.

In matters of war, Razio excelled. He'd reached the highest rank of Death Catcher before any other, and in the shortest span possible. He knew how to lead men, make difficult decisions, and find his way out of tricky situations. But in this, he was helpless.

The baby continued to scream, urine dribbling from its swaddled brown clothing. This was very bad. Any predator with half a nose would smell this and come running. He'd never considered that babies could urinate. He'd been too busy trying to detach himself from the rest of humankind to notice children or their mothers. He would have laughed had he not been so disturbed. The mount flicked its ears forward, shying away from the sound, then lowered its head to eat a mouthful of grass.

Razio snapped his fingers. That's it, food! It must be hungry! Quickly, Razio found a slice of salted pork and offered it to the infant. "Here you go. Eat this." He bit into a piece. "See? Mmm, delicious. Come on, try it."

But the baby refused to eat. Razio pinched his brow, then remembered the pack he'd taken from Voltium. He dismounted, laid the baby in the grass, and rummaged through, but found only two dozen brown cloths, a bull horn with something fleshy attached at the end, and bottled canisters.

Razio rubbed his forehead as the baby continued to scream. What had he been thinking? He understood cats better than babies, and he knew nothing about cats.

He scratched his beard. Animals. Baby animals. He'd often seen the young suckling from their mothers. They hadn't eaten solid food until they were a bit older. He stared at the screaming baby, its face red and eyes closed with the effort. Razio shook his head, then turned his gaze back to the strange items in the pack. If he didn't fix this soon, he was certain anything within a dozen leagues would hear the cries and come for them both. Razio grit his teeth with frustration.

A bull horn with a fleshy thing on it, canisters of white liquid, and two dozen cloths. He picked up the bull horn and the liquid, then snapped his fingers. It must be milk. Without its mother, the baby still had to eat, and what better way than to simulate the process. Simply ingenious.

Razio quickly unscrewed the cap, dripped half the milk into the bullhorn, then held the fleshy side—which he now assumed was a cow udder—into the baby's mouth.

Instantly, it stopped crying. Razio blew out a breath. Amazing.

His ears still rang as the infant continued suckling away. A breeze hissed past, cooling his hot face and sweaty palms. It would be dark soon, and he needed to find somewhere to hide. When the baby finished, Razio changed its cloth, trying to reverse engineer the puzzle of knots and wraps, then burned the old one. He couldn't risk leaving anything behind.

Evening came and went. The baby woke several times during the night to feed, but when morning returned, he was sound asleep. Razio rubbed his eyes, exhausted. He never imagined caring for a baby could be so difficult. He held the infant in his arms, rocking him, watching his tiny lips part as he breathed. Such a fragile treasure. Innocent features, tiny hands, delicate, twiddling toes.

Strapping the baby to his chest with a bit of rope and cloth so he'd have use of both hands, he mounted his horse and galloped away. The infant could sleep through anything. Razio rubbed his eyes again. Anything except the night.

The baby was fortunate to be so oblivious to the dangers surrounding him. "You'll be all right. You'll see." Razio rubbed the child's cheek. The baby needed no convincing, but he did.

He'd better prepare for the worst. He'd traveled far enough away that perhaps he could risk re-feeding on the dead. Razio traced a golden symbol on his cape. It translated, *Sow Duty, Reap the Harvest.* It meant something completely different now.

After touching his *Ashima* and forcing down the pain, he found another recent graveyard brimming with newly dead. He could see it on the hilltop above. Razio drained them of their sizzling, crackling power, watching the ground dip and settle as the bodies beneath turned to dust. He sighed with solace, satiated, and felt the pressure of the stolen essence expand the boundaries of his reservoir. This new burial ground had been larger than the last, and had filled him fully.

He smiled down at the sleeping baby, then curled his lip at the irony. Only the dead kept this new life flourishing. At that thought, Razio gazed out at the grasslands with resolve. Any who dared disrupt his purpose would know just how much dead he could wield.

As he raced across the countryside, the landscape soon changed from empty grasslands and wheat fields to lush forest. Morning light brightened to afternoon, then dimmed into evening, and the forest grew too dense to gallop through. He'd changed and fed the baby several times, and knew that if he didn't find help within the next couple days, the infant would have nothing left to eat except salted pork. Razio shook his head at that thought. The baby didn't even have teeth. No wonder he preferred liquid food.

After ensuring the baby remained securely strapped to his chest, he jumped off his horse and led her through the thick vines and branches, cutting through with his knife, unwilling to risk using the dead for fear of alerting any possible sentries. He wished he had a map. Seldom having traveled this far north, he couldn't be certain how soon he'd reach the border, but he couldn't be more than two days away. He'd follow the stars this night.

The baby roused from sleep and yawned, and Razio pursed his lips in a smile. As soon as the infant opened his eyes and recognized Razio, he giggled.

"That's right. I'm a funny looking man, aren't I?"

The baby giggled again. Any other would fear Razio, hardened warriors included. This child was something special.

He tickled the infant under his chin, but suddenly heard a rustling in the vines on his right flank.

Battle instincts flared to life. He jumped on his horse, and clutched the power of the dead through his *Ashima*, forcing back the pain in an instant. It left a revolting bony aftertaste in his mouth, but with senses heightened, the foliage of the forest smelled sweet and vibrant, his cape weighing heavy on his shoulders. He never liked clutching the dead so quickly.

Two arrows sang through the air from nearby dense shrubbery. Wasting no time, he incinerated them with a flick of a fingertip. He narrowed his eyes. Arrows? In a thick forest? Insulting. Whatever the attackers thought they were doing, they were fools. His body tightened with the anticipation of a fight.

Stretching out his fingers like claws, Razio lifted his arms and flicked out his power, the burning dead scorching through him. All plant life immediately surrounding him disintegrated. Previous lush trees, full shrubs, and even tall grass decayed to nothing but ash, flaking to the dead ground beneath, reeking of old, burning flesh.

But the ashen gaps in the forest exposed a near dozen soldiers surrounding him in black and gold armor—at the ready with arrows nocked to bows, and swords at their hips. Razio tensed his shoulders and grimaced, still offended by the feeble attack.

Amazingly unworried, the baby peered about the archers, curious. Razio nearly cracked a smile, but he would finish these brutes off before daring one. He patted the infant's back, readying a final spell.

"So it's true." Behind the decay, a bald rider, tattoos for eyebrows, emerged from the forest on horseback. The archers eyed him with reverence. A black cape fell from his shoulders, golden symbols embroidered upon it in abundant numbers. Jahot from the Sovereign Lands—a bureaucrat. Razio stiffened at the sight of him. He was paler than usual. The fool was addicted to power, and always stayed close to the city. He was no leader of men. What was he doing out here?

Razio touched another golden symbol emblazoned on his cape. It translated, *Inaction Breeds Perdition*. He'd learned that lesson well. "What do you and your bootlickers want, Jahot? You stand no chance with this pack. And we both know you're no leader."

Jahot patted the neck of his mount, earning a soft snort from his dark warhorse. "Perhaps that's why he chose you. You're always on edge, Razio. Always ready for a fight." He rubbed his bald head. "Just trying to get your attention, is all. Had to see if the rumors were true."

"My attention?" Razio still held the power of the dead, ready to release at a thought's notice. "You'd have better luck throwing your cape at me." Arrows. Insulting.

Jahot grinned, and his tattoos wrinkled where his eyebrows should have been. "Perhaps."

"Why are you here?"

"As I said, he's chosen you. You are to be promoted, and we have orders to ride. Our Lord is willing to forgive this little incident, as long as you deal with it here and now." His face had grown dark.

"Promoted? There is no higher rank for a Death Catcher."

"There is now. Our Lord needs one of us at his side—one who has thrived in this war and knows the land. A master strategist, a leader, but above all, one whose *Ashima* is far stronger than the rest. You are to be Seogsa—slave to none but our Lord. But you must kill this...thing to prove your loyalty, and come with me. Now." It was difficult to see, but Razio caught a hint of envy on Jahot's curled lip.

Second in command. Razio licked his teeth, letting that thought permeate in his mind, then patted the curious baby. It would have been tempting. Yes, tempting indeed. But this *little incident* was not one to be *dealt with*. This baby had a life of his own. Nobody would snatch that away. Not while he drew breath.

Thoughts of his home and country grew in his mind. It was everything he knew. But now, it repulsed him. He nearly spat.

Razio held the baby tighter. "Interesting, how this position should be offered to me now." He took a moment to glare. "I've chosen my path. Move aside."

Jahot paused to rub his tattoos and smile. "You must know, I am our Lord's second choice." He smirked. "Seems we both know our fates. Thank you, Razio, for forcing my hand. I alone deserve that title." His dark expression turned murderous and hungry. "Now, I mustn't wait to kill you."

Jahot snapped his fingers, and two other Death Catchers emerged from the tree line atop horseback, stepping through the soot. Their capes hadn't near as many symbols, but if they were traveling with Jahot, they were powerful. Razio tapped his fingers with his thumbs, preparing the dead, his skin growing hot with the thrill before battle. Now he knew why the archers were here. To distract him from these two. He furrowed his eyebrows as annoyance flared to anger.

How dare they threaten his child's life? Razio glanced down at the baby as the two others joined Jahot on either side. He'd never felt this protective or more connected to anything. Perhaps because the infant needed him. Or perhaps it was Razio who needed this child. He rubbed the back of the baby's head, then returned his anger to the battlefield.

They'd set him up perfectly, waited until he became stuck in these dense woods. To escape, he'd need to waste his power decaying trees to clear the way for his mount, and simultaneously, combat the archers and three Death Catchers—all while protecting the baby. No, he couldn't run this time. He needed to make his stand here. There was no other chance to keep the baby alive.

With a clawed grasp, Razio twisted his hand, encircling the weakest of the Death Catchers with a fog, then in an instant, concentrated that fog on his heart. The Death Catcher gasped, fell off his horse, and disintegrated.

One down. It was a sneaky move that bypassed newer Death Catchers' defenses, but the stronger two wouldn't be caught so unaware.

Jahot's eyes widened with rage. "Fire!"

Razio redirected the arrows with a wave of his hand towards the other Death Catcher. It was all the fool could do to avoid them.

But Jahot had already freed the dead with a spell. Razio's hands steamed. The hair on his arms and face burned, his throat suddenly dry and cracking with blisters. He shot a worried gaze at the baby as the scorching pain threatened to sear him from inside out. He would have screamed if he had time, but his defenses reacted to the attack, draining much of his reservoir, and restoring him to health. Now, only a tingling numbness remained of the pain, and the baby remained untouched.

He growled in anger. If they killed him, Razio knew they'd turn their rage on the baby, fulfilling his contract. He wouldn't let that happen.

As the Death Catcher recovered from the arrows, Razio spooked the archers' horses with Whispers of the dead. He soothed his own mount as they whinnied and neighed, bucked the archers off with unnatural force, trampled them to death, then galloped at the two remaining Death Catchers.

They barely had time to react, forcing the horses rampaging into the deep woods with Whispers of their own.

He was surprised the child didn't scream. Only startled, the baby gazed up, latched onto Razio's neck, and nibbled on his beard, maintaining that trusting, dependent expression. But Razio couldn't afford to risk spending time soothing the infant. He clenched his jaw, narrowed his eyes, and turned his remaining reservoir on the Death Catchers. No more holding back.

He released the raw power of the dead, a freezing chill shooting from his chest to fingertips. It leapt out in darkness and burning fog, overpowering the weaker Death Catcher, dropping him to the ground. He screamed in agony, clawing at his disintegrating face as Jahot struggled to hold back the torrent.

The fool managed to stay atop his horse, but Razio pushed the powers of the dead harder. His hands shook. Sweat dripped down the back of his neck. His muscles ached with the struggle. But little by little, the dead inched closer to Jahot, swirling about in angry swells of mist and shadow.

At the last moment, Jahot screamed with rage. The powers of the dead consumed him, but not before he lashed out with a final burst of his own. It whipped out with shadowy tendrils and latched onto Razio's arm, squeezing, burning, scorching into his very bone.

His defenses depleted, Razio hissed in agony as Jahot fell to ash. He struggled to control the damage with the little dead he had left, but those black tendrils dug deeper, only finally dissipating with the last measure of his reservoir.

Drained and bleary, Razio fell off his horse, holding the infant close as he hit the ashen ground.

3 THE CHARGE

He awoke coughing, arm screaming in burning agony, baby asleep. Deep crevices blackened his arm to the bone. His head buzzed with weakness. He needed to re-feed on the dead. Slowly, Razio touched his Ashima. The agony came in a torrent, weakening him even more. He shivered with pain. His arm felt like a separate entity, torturing him to the point of breaking. Gasping, Razio suppressed a scream, barely hanging on to his Ashima.

But his senses flooded with clarity. The after-scent of burnt flesh still hung in the air, now more vile, forcing his nose to itch. The blackness now seemed to be ripping his arm apart, tendon by tendon.

And the baby needed to be changed.

Razio grunted with revulsion, then touched the dead archers with his Ashima, sucking in their crackling power, watching their bones flake to dust. A shame the Death Catchers were already ash. They would have replenished him fully. The archers had only pressurized a fraction of his reservoir, and he used that to tame the pain of his wound.

He drew in a breath, then reached out farther, struggling to find another burial ground not already consumed. Razio shook his head in anger. The Death Catchers he'd killed must have sucked everything dry for leagues.

Reaching out farther still, he felt his Ashima thin, stretching to its limits. He was stronger than most, but even he struggled against the boundary of his power, searching, grasping for anything.

Ah, he barely felt it. A near imperceptible tingle. Just outside his reach. After wrapping his arm thick with poultice, he changed and fed the baby, burned the cloth, then led his horse north, towards the graveyard. Towards the border.

He struggled nearly a league through the thick forest before he could properly re-feed, bit by insects, slapping at mosquitoes, dodging spiders and pepper ants. Now it was evening, and he would need to spend another night in this dense forest.

But that fact only renewed his determination. He'd been given his final chance, offered promotion to Second in the growing empire. He believed Jahot now. It was the envious, but earnest way he'd said it. All this he would receive, if only he would murder a baby.

Razio sniffed, glancing down at the precious gift in his arms. There was no choice. The child's life was his only motivation.

Using a wisp of the dead, he cleaned his path free of scent and rubble, reset his wards and defenses, pacified his flaring wound—which for some reason he could not heal—then released his Ashima and fell asleep with the baby.

Morning came in a rush. He awoke to a giggling infant gripping his cheeks with its tiny fingernails. Razio held his hands away, then laughed. "Early riser, hmm? Let's get you fed."

The sun had not fully risen. Cool breezes caressed his face and tickled his spine, stars growing dimmer as the moon receded. But the pain hadn't dimmed.

Razio winced against his burning wound. He changed the dressings only to find it worse. Boils and lesions burrowed inside the black crevices, the veins up to his shoulder had darkened, presumably poisoned. He could barely flex his fingers. What had Jahot done to him?

It was as if Nightsweeper, from her realm below, had lent Jahot her essence. Razio shook his head. It was something he always feared. Something all Death Catchers feared. All dead souls wandered the Lost Winds, but their bodies belonged to Nightsweeper. Death Catchers had too often touched the power of the dead, and it hadn't gone unnoticed.

More reason to get the baby to safety, and quickly. He hadn't a clue if he'd even survive this wound. And thinking back, Jahot had seemed pale—

even for him. Perhaps a side effect of Nightsweeper's touch.

After grasping his agonizing Ashima, he did what he could with the wound, using too much of his reservoir. The black veins receded, the boils dissipated, but the new lesions inside the black crevices wouldn't close. Razio sighed. At this rate, he'd need to re-feed again before noon. And so close to the border, he wasn't sure he should risk holding his Ashima. He had to be less than a day away. The episode from yesterday surely would have drawn in Creators. But then again, he needed to find them.

He'd found a reason to live. The child had opened his eyes to the potential of a different future. One with the possibility of settling down. Razio chuckled despite his pain. A Death Catcher settling down. What a ridiculous notion.

After eating, then feeding and changing the baby, he led his horse north until the forest grew less dense. The wound continued pulsing deep, burning pain to his shoulder, and now the top of his chest ached with the same burn.

Razio grunted, then stopped to rest and change the poultice. The baby was sound asleep. Razio was tempted to wake him just to see that joyful, life-bearing smile. But no, better to take care of his arm and be on his way to safety as quickly as possible.

His arm convulsed and burned as the wrappings fell off. His fingertips had turned completely black, and those dark, aggressive veins now stretched to the top of his chest like spider's web. Razio held his breath, fearful to touch his Ashima, for he knew how much more pain it would bring. But he reached for it anyway.

And shivered with icy shock. The torment drowned out every other heightened sense. It twisted and scorched inside, slithering throughout his arm and shoulder like a living entity. Razio fell to the ground and arched his back, but protected the baby by holding him tightly to his chest. He took the brunt of the shock when he landed on his spine, tensing every muscle in his body, struggling not to scream from the unbearable agony.

With the fraction of his mind not consumed by the torment, Razio directed the flow of dead into the wound, to numb the pain, to force back the darkness that would otherwise consume him. With shallow breaths, Razio concentrated harder, and the pain turned into a dull throb. His fingertips regained some of their color, and the black spider web of veins retreated back to the top of his shoulder. But try as he might, he could not force it back further.

With his reservoir nearly depleted, the pressure of the dead nearly gone, Razio decided he must maintain a constant flow into the wound if he had any chance of survival. At this rate, he wouldn't last another day. He squeezed his eyes shut, then studied the lesions before wrapping his arm with fresh poultice. He could barely move his fingers, but when he did, the black crevices inside his arm exposed the tendons as they flexed. But at least he could feel his fingertips. There was hope, for now, as long as he continuously touched his Ashima, and found enough dead to harness.

Ensuring the baby remained securely strapped to his chest, Razio mounted his horse, and rode through the forest, slowing only to re-feed and redirect the dead to his wound. He shook his head. With so much consumed, he would alert any Death Catcher or Creator within a dozen leagues. He needed to ride faster, and hope the Creators found him before his own brethren. It was the baby's only chance to survive. He hoped his horse could maintain the pace.

Razio ducked down on his mount, trees and shrubs blowing by in a haze, and continued the flow into his arm. But with the concentration it required, let alone lack of sleep, exhaustion set in. He re-fed every few leagues as the evening turned dark. There would be no rest this night.

Following the stars above, he raced through the thinning forest until it waned into green pasture–thick with long, wispy grass saddle high. Though the sky remained cloudless, the thin moon helped conceal Razio's course. Provisions thinning, hunger and thirst weighed him down.

The aroma of fresh mint heavy on the midnight breeze, the baby finally woke. The child peered up, and although Razio knew the infant was hungry just by that expression, the babe didn't cry out. Razio allowed himself to smile. The infant trusted him, depended on him even. He'd never before felt such devotion, such care, such comfort from anyone. At first sight of the baby, Razio knew the child needed protection, but it was more than that now. Emotion he'd never felt before had consumed his heart. And he didn't know what to do with it.

The burning pain of his wound subdued, he reined in his mount to a trot, then fed and changed the infant while on horseback. His fingers had frozen black, and he only had use of one hand. Razio grimaced and rubbed his eyes with exhaustion, struggling not to spill the canister as he dumped it into the bull horn.

As soon as the baby began eating, Razio yawned, struggling to keep his eyes open. But he was now in the grasslands, and it wouldn't be long before he reached the border. Just in time, too. The baby had only two remaining canisters of milk. Razio brushed a hand through his thick locks. If he survived his wound long enough to ensure the baby's safety, maybe, just maybe, he would learn firsthand of the Creators legendary healing powers—if they granted him mercy. And that was a big if.

If that unlikely possibility became reality, everything would change. He would care for the baby as his own. Learn how to tend to his needs properly. Raise the child never to make his mistakes. Razio glanced at the infant and smiled. He could see it now. Perhaps he could take up farming in a distant town to the north, or pick up a trade. Anything to keep this child living and growing strong.

With determination renewed, Razio narrowed his eyes and rode hard through the night, stopping only to care for the baby and rest his mount. He re-fed on the dead, trying to limit how far Nightsweeper's touch spread. But try as he might, those black veins stretched to his neck, past his chest, then crossed to his other shoulder, burning worse with every moment of progression. Razio gulped down the agony and exhaustion, but his head grew faint, and his vision started to blur.

His horse near frothing, his wound pulsating, the baby still sleeping, the shadows and silence of night dissipated as the first light of morning brushed warmth across his cheek.

At those new rays, Razio tensed, sensing a vibrant crackling power. He reined in his mount just before the crest of a ridge, and squeezed his reins in alarm. He couldn't see anything yet, but he didn't need to.

Death Catchers. Dozens. Razio tapped the fingers of his good hand together. They had tried to mask their power, but nobody could hide such an immense measure of the dead.

He drummed his toes inside his boots with apprehension, and glanced at the baby. There was no way he could protect the infant from this. How had they ridden so quickly?

Razio rubbed the back of the baby's head. This had to be the border. It didn't matter how the Death Catchers had arrived before him, it only mattered that they had. As impossible as the odds were, he needed to find a way to usher this child to safety.

Letting his exhausted mount graze, Razio jumped off and grimaced when he landed, the pulsating burn of the wound searing through his flesh at the impact. Ducking low, he struggled through the deep grass, gritting his teeth with every step. At the peak of the ridge, he bobbed his head up just long enough to see what lay ahead.

He immediately ducked back down and cursed. Every Death Catcher he knew of must be down there. And Creators. Lots of Creators. Old men with beards and graying women looked on with obvious nervousness. In their robes of green, red, black, white, or brown, they stood at the peak of the next knoll in disorganized, awkward lines, studying the Death Catchers at the bottom of the slope—who outnumbered them two to one. These Creators were not accustomed to battle. They didn't stand a chance.

Razio pursed his lips. Only the soft snort of a mount, the hiss of wind slicing through the glades disturbed the stillness. That moment of peace before death. Razio clenched the fist of his good hand. All mounted on horseback, the Death Catchers flexed their hands, glaring, the breeze rolling through their black capes. All held themselves with confidence, a breath away from battle.

But none paid attention to him or the dead he commanded. He shook his head, then stared down at the child. He woke just moments before, and gazed up at Razio with a loving smile. In spite of himself, he couldn't help but smile back.

This infant had somehow managed to infect Razio with his innocence and life. He had grown attached to the baby. No, it was more than that. A deeper connection, a bond he presumed only parents could feel. A fondness, a warmth, a care for this child.

Love.

Razio touched his lips and blinked, chills whispering down his back. He'd never known love. Now to admit that he did in fact love this child, it was more reward than he'd ever known. No gold or duty, no patriotism, no bond of death compared.

He'd thought redemption improbable, but now it didn't matter. Regardless what he felt for this child, how attached he'd become, how much he needed this infant, Razio would see this through to the end. He would sacrifice all if it meant this child would live.

Razio checked his reservoir, and finding the pressure of the dead near full, calmed himself with a deep breath, then mounted his horse and trotted down the crest. The baby looked only at him, that loving and dependent gaze locked on his eyes. He hoped he knew what he was doing.

Turning his attention to the Death Catchers below, Razio calmed his emotions, and cut off the flow of dead into his wound. He needed every measure of power he could wield, and had to block the pain with only his mind.

He rode down the grassy knoll, eyes of stone resolve, the Death

Catchers turning to stare. And then it clicked.

It now made sense why Tynza was willing to forgive his betrayal. When Razio had found the baby, the Death Catcher who killed his men must have had orders to ride to the border to mount this attack. But Razio had left with the infant before the Death Catcher had a chance to deliver the orders. Razio continued riding toward the ranks of Death Catchers, ignoring their sneers and glares. They'd all had advance notice to ride to the border for this battle, which was why they'd arrived so quickly.

And he'd killed three at his last encounter. Fortunately, there was no way those gathered here knew of such betrayal. Regardless of those glares, they would assume he was here to join their lines. Baby or no baby. Contract or no contract.

He slid through their ranks, ignoring their disdainful stares, their unenlightened hatred.

"Come to redeem yourself?" The lead Death Catcher crossed his arms and sneered, clicking his black, dagger-like fingernails on his chest, and stared at the baby.

Razio narrowed his eyes, then recognized in the crowd the Death Catcher who'd killed his men. He must have told the others of Razio's betrayal. He cursed under his breath.

He only had one chance at this. Now at their front, he wheeled his mount around and halted, holding the baby close, bearing the most intimidating glare he could muster. "Redemption?" He had to bear down harder on his grimace to keep from laughing at the absurdity. "I have no need for redemption. I admit I arrived late, but I come bearing a gift." He indicated the child. "Let all these Creators know first-hand what happens to those who dare oppose us."

The Death Catcher tapped his black fingernails again and sniffed with disgust. The others looked to him with deference, but the same disgust and derision of the baby lined their dark expressions. "Want to convince us, traitor? Hand that…creature…over. Now. Then we'll talk."

"No." Razio found himself almost growling. "I will ride forward, raise this child high, and stick my knife in its throat for all the Creators to see. If that won't convince you, or them, of my resolve, then take my life, as I am no longer deserving of it." Razio tried keeping his disgust for his own words internalized, but feared his emotion had bled out.

The Death Catcher narrowed his eyes and curled his lip, then nodded. He didn't trust Razio, but then, what Death Catcher trusted anyone? Razio didn't bother analyzing further. He turned his mount back around, then slowly marched up the hill towards the Creators.

He glanced down at the baby, who smiled with a curious, but unworried gaze. This child implicitly trusted his judgment. Razio found himself relaxing slightly at the confidence, and held himself high as he approached the Creators.

They tensed at his approach, tightening their knuckles, narrowing their eyes, readying spells. They grouped more closely together, forming unpracticed ranks, but ready for a fight.

Not a dozen paces away, Razio held his breath, then unstrapped the baby and held him up high with his good arm, trying his best to control the pain in his other.

He used a wave of his power to amplify his voice forward, and sever it from behind. "Hear my words." His voice sounded stronger and more confident than he felt. "Do with me what you will, but do not let harm come to this child."

Razio's breath caught in his throat. He'd known he was willing to sacrifice himself, but to hear the words from his own mouth bore the sentiment into stone. The Death Catchers' glares and anticipation burrowed with hatred into his back.

The Creators glanced at each other, confused, but still at the ready. Razio finally reined in his mount a few paces away from their front lines. He'd interrupted this battle mere moments before it started.

Razio flinched, the pain of his wound too much to bear.

The black veins had snaked halfway down his good arm. Before his muscles gave out, he lowered the baby and hugged him close.

It was all he could do not to cry out in agony. The touch of Nightsweeper had eaten away most of his body. It boiled and burned from inside. Razio grinded his teeth together. He needed to maintain his façade of control these last few moments. He was grateful for his horse, certain he could no longer walk.

"What is this, Death Rider? A peace offering?" A tall, sinewy Creator garbed in green robes folded his hands and frowned, his tapering eyes casting an unusual glower. "No child's life is traded as currency. Not here."

Razio scratched his beard. Yes, he'd made the right decision. He summoned his strength, and said, "I offer no peace between us, but you must protect this child." His voice cracked with the struggle of his next words. "Please, care for him. I no longer have the strength. He needs more than I can give." Razio blinked away tears forming in his eyes. He hadn't foreseen such conflicting emotions. "In the briefest of moments, he has rendered more light than I ever deserve. I cherish him as my own. He must live. He is the beacon in this shadowy world."

Razio swallowed back his passion as the sinewy Creator in green strode forward. His glare had softened, his tapered eyes thoughtful. He reached up a lanky hand to Razio's arm, and asked, "What is his name?"

Razio furrowed his brow. Name? He'd never even considered it. He glanced across the whispering glades, reflecting upon the question, still feeling the heat of the Death Catchers' glares behind him. He would never name the baby after himself. Nobody should bear that burden. He considered his father, and mother. No, he needed to choose one not associated with this horrid empire. Razio gritted his teeth as the pain continued to tear his body apart. He shivered, struggling to hold it at bay, his blurry vision dimming and light head swimming.

Then it came to him. He turned his shaky head to the Creator, and after ensuring his voice shield to the Death Catchers remained intact, said, "I name him after my grandfather–the only man I knew with a heart. I name him Cremoré."

The Creator nodded, then narrowed his eyes, studying Razio's black veins and damaged body. "Val, come here. Look at this." He gave the Death Catchers a worried glare.

A Creator in white with long, brown hair stepped forward. When the other showed her the wounds, she covered her mouth, suppressing alarm. "How long?"

Razio shrugged. "Not two days."

Her eyes widened with shock. "Two days? You shouldn't be alive." She shook her head, tracing the blackness back to his deadened arm. "I cannot heal this. Perhaps if you came to us sooner..."

She trailed off and Razio nodded. He hadn't expected to survive. But perhaps he could give Cremoré one final offering. The baby deserved a full life, a chance to choose his destiny. These Creators could care for him far better, though it pained him to admit. It was time to let go. Time to choose his own destiny.

The Death Catchers behind were growing anxious, pointing and plotting. The tension mounting, he knew any moment they would lose their patience, then turn all life to dust. He needed to act quickly. But he also needed his strength. "Can you numb the pain?"

She studied the black veins once more. "I'll do what I can."

The moment she closed her eyes, the blackness began receding. Razio shook as she fought against the darkness, pushing back the burning torment, the agony. Her brow furrowed with concentration, Val brushed her delicate fingers across his skin, shooting chills throughout his body. He closed his eyes as the pain diminished and his vision cleared, as his exhaustion waned, as his strength returned. She knew what he was going to do. They all did.

The Creators looked on with hope for the first time. Hope in him. Hope in death to preserve life. But Razio's only concern was the child. Only by preserving the babe's life would Razio find peace.

When Val released him, he opened his eyes with newfound vigor, and flexed his fists—both of them. The stinging darkness still weaved up through his wound, growing slowly, but only a dull throbbing remained. She appeared exhausted. Razio whispered, "Thank you."

Val nodded, slightly pale, and fell back in the ranks. Razio returned his attention to the Creator in front of him, and hugged the baby one last time. His heart ached with the burden of his decision. But it was the only choice he could make. Cremoré looked up and smiled, that infectious love warming where the pain used to be. "You be good, now."

Razio leaned forward, kissed the child, and handed him to the Creator. Then with that loss, Razio narrowed his eyes, a well of pain, regret, and emptiness churning to the surface of his glare. "Take care of him, or I promise—I'll return from the Lost Winds with the wrath of the Nameless One."

Judging by the Creator's shock, it was a sentiment anyone could have believed. Razio quickly handed over the child. It had the reaction he'd expected. The Death Catchers furiously shouted, whipping out their arms to release spells, enraged by such a deep betrayal. They aligned themselves in tight formations, but the Creators had found new vigor, clenching their teeth and flexing their fists, leaning forward and whispering to ready their own spells.

Razio turned his horse around with stone resolve and a warm heart, and checked the pressure of his reservoir. Yes, he had enough. One final attack. He would take out as many as he could before drifting to the Lost Winds. As many as needed to switch the odds and ensure the baby's survival.

With a roar that could frighten the gods, Razio ripped off his cape, dug his heels into his horse, and charged the battlefield.

ABOUT THE AUTHOR

Matt lives in the Denver, CO area with his lovely family and three felines. He is currently employed at a major telecommunications company and is working towards his Bachelor of Science in Business Administration – Concentration in Finance. When he's not playing with children, writing, studying, or working, he visits the gym five days per week or catches a movie. However, his love of the craft will never fail. He plans on writing until all matter turns to dust. Let old age never claim his soul.